THE
BREAK

&

A NOVELETTE

ERICA SAND

A reminder to the dark, dry days
that there is perfection, occasionally.

Table of Contents

CHAPTER ONE

"SATU"

The golden year of good luck for Jenny began in the summer. It had started, somewhat surprisingly, in Indonesia.

"Are you fucking kidding me?" Jenny said, grabbing the two Garuda airline tickets from the man's sweaty hand.

Two years ago…, Jenny thought as she held the damp tickets in her fist, thinking wryly of the nightmare these trips had been in the past. But this time, standing in that tiny airport in Medan, Jenny felt a golden glow pleasantly embrace her, creating an aura of possibilities. She knew, deep into her bones, that the next month was going to be fantastic, and she gave a fist pump as the Garuda airline tickets flapped back and forth in her hand like a trophy of flowers.

"No way," Steph drawled in her Australian accent, wrinkling up her eyes as she smiled.

"Two tickets to Jauh *and* it only took ten minutes. Ten minutes!" Jenny let out a triumphant smile as Steph's eyes locked onto the tickets in disbelief.

Letting out a smoker's chuckle, Steph cupped her hand around Jenny's waist, the slimmest dip it had been in years. Jenny loved the way anything she wore fit her new trim body. She could distinctly feel her bones and muscles smoothly underneath a fine layer of skin—so much better than digging her hands through body fat to reach her frame. She had even worn horizontal stripes for the first time in years; it gave her a trendy look now and didn't make her look wider in an unbecoming way.

The thing was, getting airline tickets in mere minutes for a flight that was leaving in less than an hour had never happened before, back when the girls had been working in Indonesia. They had been in Sumatra's sweaty armpit of a capital city many times as they had plane-hopped between Aceh and Jauh. The small island of Jauh, one they frequented on every break, hosted one of the best surf breaks in the world, followed a Christian religion in contrast to the Muslim area they lived in (so actually served alcohol and allowed them to wear bikinis and sundresses), and had its own unique culture.

Even though Jauh was only a short plane ride from the largest island of Sumatra in Indonesia, transportation had always been a nightmare. Before returning to Indonesia, Jenny had already prepared herself for the anticipated chaotic traffic, breathing in heavy pollution, and sweating profusely in the small airport while the whirring of the air conditioners pumped out only hot, stale air with yellowed walls sticky with smoke from the hundreds of men puffing cigarettes at tables five feet away from the "non-smoking" section.

But, mysteriously, since Steph and Jenny had met up in Singapore for this reunion trip, everything had just been so *easy*. Jenny had flown down from Kuwait after finishing up a year-long teaching contract, and Steph had come up from her beach house in Australia. They had shrieked with joy at the sight of one another, bought a few bottles of duty-free vodka, and caught up, talking nonstop on the flight to Indonesia. The prompt tickets to their tiny surf destination were the rare cherry on top.

"I still cannot believe our luck," Steph said as she lit up a cigarette.

"Yes, we are in for an amazing holiday."

Jenny put on her backpack, and they walked towards their gate, which, ironically, had fresh white paint on the walls and an air conditioner that cranked out cold air. The two girls looked at each other and let out a laugh.

ဆ

"A ride to the surf break for 200,000 rupees!" The tiny Indonesian man wore his black baseball hat backwards, and a half-finished tattoo of a sunset or sunrise trailed down his forearm. Steph warmed to him immediately.

"What's your name, and how long is the trip?" Steph spat out the two-pronged question in one go as she wanted to move through the little throng of porters and drivers as quickly as possible. She was still fresh with the rush of seeing her friend again and was trying not to get frustrated with the onslaught of barters.

"Adi, and it takes two hours to get there."

Taken aback by his direct answers, Steph sucked in her breath. Most barters would have asked a question back, such as, *Oh, are you from Australia?* Or any other conversation starters. This was just answer-answer.

Finally, her brain worked out a response. "It usually takes at least five hours," she said, looking questioningly at Adi.

He shrugged his shoulders, and the sun grew larger on his arm—definitely a sunrise. "Road is fixed now."

Well, I'll be damned.

"Jenny, we are going with Adi." Steph nodded in Adi's direction through the mass of other porters, who were still yelling questions at the girls in a simultaneous uproar. Adi's quietness, which appeared more like boredom, stood out louder than any of the other noisy porters who were jumping around in animated circles trying to grab the luggage out of Steph's hands. Adi lit up a cigarette and winked at her. *Well, I guess he's not that bored,* Steph thought, blushing involuntarily.

Jenny smiled at Steph. "Did he say *two hours?*"

Glancing up, Steph saw that Adi was looking the other direction and rubbing his eye—the one that had winked at her. She suddenly paled. Had he even winked? He probably just had something in his eye...or maybe he was just shy. She shrugged to herself. Even this mishap couldn't break the good luck trajectory. "Yes, he did," she answered Jenny, "and I can't believe it. First, the quick tickets, and now, only two hours to get down to the break?"

"Well, I'll be fucked." Jenny let out a whistle.

Although small, Adi was strong, and he scooped up their backpacks in one movement. Once the other porters saw that the Western women had selected someone, they ran off and promptly started harassing the other passengers. Steph let out a deep breath and felt the tension release from her shoulders. The claustrophobia brought on by the humidity and the sheer number of people in Indonesia always made her feel an ironic mixture of stress and energy. It was like her nervous system lit up with fight and flight at the same time, giving her both an upper and a downer. Man, she loved Indonesia. To Steph, just being there was the best natural drug ever.

She thought back to the last time she and Jenny had been to Jauh. It was right after their contract had ended in Aceh, the province they had worked on in Sumatra, and they had taken their last surf holiday together with Audrey. It had been so much more difficult before, so soon after the Asian Tsunami. Apparently, little Jauh had really picked up some tourism since then and fixed the road down to the famed surf break.

As they followed Adi outside, the wind kicked up Jenny's blonde hair into a flame. It was still so surreal to see Jenny that Steph reflexively reached out her hand and stroked Jenny's hair down. A simple move, but one that seemed to connect her to Jenny and make this entire trip seem real.

As they settled into Adi's van, he immediately lit up a joint and turned up the music. AC/DC coupled with the sweet smell of marijuana flooded the car.

"This is the life," Jenny said, putting on her sunglasses.

Steph couldn't agree more. *This is going to be the golden summer,* Steph thought as Adi reached back and handed her the joint while "Back in Black" blared out of the speakers.

୫୦

On the way to the surf break, Jenny and Steph had stopped to pee. It was another popular surf spot near the break—about twenty minutes away from the guest houses. When Jenny had run into Mason, a gorgeous surfer, Steph had watched comically as they'd introduced themselves before muttering something about forgetting something in the van and quickly walking away.

Mason's eyes were almost a turquoise green, and Jenny couldn't stop smiling. Maybe it was the weed, but she thought it was probably the way he kept flirtatiously looking her up and down. His attention stroked her nerves deliciously, making the hairs on her arms stand on end. In an effort to seem more casual, she crossed her arms, then remembered that she had read somewhere that crossing your arms was a stance of non-invitation. She dropped her hands quickly, and they swung down and abruptly hit her thighs. Trying to cover the move, she began thumping her thighs in little beats, but then she realized she was drumming to no apparent music. So she started humming a little tune. *Man, I'm stoned,* she thought as she couldn't think of a song to hum apart from *Back in Black,* which was a very hard song to hum.

She couldn't even remember the last time she had gotten high. It must've been…*before Kuwait?* she thought to herself. Kuwait was a dry country— well, it was only "officially" a dry country as the black market was booming with booze, but regardless, there was no weed around.

For this holiday, she was determined to have a fantastic time and let loose. Once she started graduate school in the fall, it was going to be books and tight purse strings, so this was her moment.

Mason had introduced himself mere minutes before, and he let out an amused smile as his eyes stopped following her nervous movements and instead rested on hers. Jenny was still drumming the awkward song, distracted now by thoughts about graduate school, but when Mason connected eyes with her, she was pulled back to the present. And what a juicy present moment. She let her gaze trail down his torso, and even though he was sitting down, his six pack abs were perfectly intact like a...

"So, where are you guys staying?" Mason asked in his rough but charming Australian accent.

"Um, we were planning on staying at Auntie Lorrie's place. It's where we usually stay," Jenny said.

Jenny noticed Mason's abs dance a little as he leaned forward. "Well, Adi has the best place on the beach. It's right in front of the break, and it is super laid back. He even lets me use his bike." Mason nodded towards the road where a scooter rested against a coconut tree.

"Wow, that really does sound nice," Jenny murmured amiably. "I really like him, too. He is the most straightforward guy I've ever met."

Jenny bit her lip so she wouldn't end up with a wide grin on her face again. But instead, her gaze landed back on Mason's perfectly shaped abs. She wondered what they would look like if he was standing up...or while he was lying on top of her...or—*Oh, crap, am I licking my lips?*

"Well, you should definitely stay at Adi's. It is the best place on the beach— you can have a beachfront room! Plus, me and my mates are staying there." He let out a sheepish grin, and Jenny couldn't believe her continued luck.

"Alright, we will be sure to check it out. I'd better get back now. See you around." Jenny gave a shy smile as she walked away and nearly tripped over a small rock on the windy path. Involuntarily, a little giggle escaped her lips, but she knew the sound was drowned out by the loud waves. Jenny glanced up at Steph, who was standing in front of the van, looking back and forth between Jenny and Mason with a bewildered expression on her face.

"You're hooking up with a guy before we even get there?" Steph asked as soon as Jenny got back to the van. She felt like it had taken her five minutes to cross the short distance as she had been careful not to trip over any more rocks.

She ignored her friend's teasing question. "Mason said that he and his friends are staying at Adi's guesthouse, and it is the best one on the beach. He said we should really stay there." Jenny knew she was babbling, but she couldn't help it; the weed intermingled with the flirting was making her feel like a teenager.

"Did he, now?" Steph said and lit up a cigarette. "I only saw you two checking each other out. All I have to say is that, on this Indonesian trip, you'd better get laid."

"Hey, now!" Jenny pushed her friend playfully. "Just because I didn't have a 'fifteen' moment doesn't mean I didn't have fun."

"Oh, shit." Steph let out a laugh and then groaned. "I had forgotten about that. I still can't believe I had sex with someone fifteen years younger than me! At least he was nineteen…*and* at least I got laid."

"Well, I'm sure you will have no problem with that on this trip."

Steph opened her mouth to tease Jenny more but then dropped her jaw when she followed Jenny's gaze. Another hot guy—a little older, but still with a perfect surfer body—had joined up with Mason. Adi walked over to where the guys were all talking, looking up at the girls from time to time. Jenny strained her ears, but all she could hear was the waves pounding on the reef.

"I wonder what they are saying…," Steph said.

Mason let out a laugh as Adi handed him something. *Probably some of this killer weed,* Jenny thought.

"I can't hear a thing except the waves. And a strange buzzing sound," Jenny said.

"Yeah, I hear it too. It's like there's a beat, and—oh, wait. That's the music from the van. It's just turned way down."

Both the girls started to giggle as Adi rejoined them.

"*Bagus*, let's go!" he yelled out in a voice that seemed much too loud to come from his small frame.

"Alright!" Jenny jumped in the backseat next to Steph. "Hey, Adi, do you have any more rooms available at your losmen?"

৪০

The view of the wave *was* better from this angle, even as dusk settled quickly across the horizon, blending the ocean and sky into the same expanse. Steph set down her Bintang beer on the wooden table and snuck a look at Jenny. "Auntie Lorrie is going to kill us."

Jenny stuck out her tongue in the direction of the Auntie Lorrie's losmen, and both girls let out a laugh. The last part of the sunset cast a shadow across the arch of beach where about 12 guesthouses, known as *losmens*, were perched.

"I know, but you have to admit Adi's balcony has a better view...all around," Jenny said, gesturing with her beer up around the table where, a few minutes ago, Mason and Ian had been sitting.

Auntie Lorrie's losmen was where they had stayed the previous two times they'd visited Jauh: once, during the Muslim holiday Eid al-Fitr, when they'd had leave work, and then once at the end of their contract before they had parted ways back to their own countries. Steph had returned to Australia and Jenny to America.

Jauh was an interesting place, known for rivalry and the most aggressive sales techniques that Steph had ever seen. The island itself was far off the beaten path—even for surfers—yet it had one of the best waves for surfing in the world. Because of its geographic isolation, Jauh was spared the typical tourists and instead boasted an interesting mix of professional surfers, who would stay for about a month at a time. These were serious dudes who came to surf. They were not in Jauh to party—that was reserved for Bali. Jauh was where the morning, day, and evening consisted of surfing.

Of course, a few local Bintang beers here and there or an occasional joint were necessary commodities, but there were no bars or nightlife on this quiet and remote stretch of beach. The pool house was the only "nightlife" out here, and that was a just a bamboo shack with a couple of pool tables where mostly locals would hang out. The action was the waves, and the losmens were where people would eat, sleep, and have a smoke.

These losmens were perched upon high stilts of wood with wide balconies decorated with basic commodities of hammocks and large wooden tables. Of course, there were no air conditioning or amenities in the losmens. For showers, the bathrooms had porcelain squares filled with water with a plastic bucket—"bucket showers"—and most bathrooms included a squat toilet. But you couldn't beat the price if you could afford to get to Jauh. Rooms ranged from $2 to $3 per night, not including the cost of food.

That was why the losmen owners were so crazy. They did everything they could to get you to buy your meals from them to increase their revenues, and it had become a kind of social etiquette. You ate where you stayed. If you went to someone else's losmen to eat, then you had to face hours of interrogation from your losmen owner. It was an hour of "What did you buy? How much was it? Isn't mine better? Why do you do that to me?" It was unthinkable to sleep at one losmen and then mosey on down the beach to another one for a meal. Your losmen owner would take it personally.

Where you slept was where you had coffee, beer, and food…and it was also where you bought magazines, had massages, socialized, and bought cigarettes and joints. Occasionally, there would be a bonfire party, or some losmen owner would curate a projector and show a movie, but most days, you were at your losmen or in the water on a surfboard. It was easy to see why Steph and Jenny were usually the only Western girls staying on Jauh.

Steph knew that Jenny was right, but she was always the kind of person who would stick up for the underdog. She felt like Auntie Lorrie was the underdog in this situation...*there is no way she can compete with Adi's*, thought Steph. Auntie Lorrie's losmen was boring; the girls had never had co-ed capability and had to endure Auntie Lorrie's kids making noises way too early in the morning or during afternoon hammock naps.

"She's already sent her kids over with three messages," Steph said, letting out a small whimper.

"We need to stay strong, Steph. I mean, even the Bintang is colder here." Jenny took a swig off her beer and over-exaggerated a swallow. "We can't just go to her place because we feel bad. It is *our* holiday reunion."

Jenny made sense, but Steph couldn't help feeling like they were making a mistake—like Auntie Lorrie might put a crazy hex on them or something. She was about to argue some more—if for nothing else than to at least make herself feel like she'd stood up for Auntie Lorrie. But then Ian walked back out onto the patio.

"Hi, ladies. Having a beer, I see," Ian drawled out. His tall muscular frame was intimidating in an exciting way, and Steph took another drink of beer to distract herself from staring at him. As if sensing her uneasiness, he pulled up a chair next to her and sat down, his thighs barely touching her own.

"Ah, yeah, cheers," she said, holding up her bottle.

Ian held up his empty hands, but then, as if on cue, Mason walked up and placed a beer in his palm.

"Thanks, mate," Ian said and reached down, clinking Steph's beer.

Mason grabbed a plastic chair and moved it between Ian and Jenny. Sitting down, he propped his feet up on the wooden table.

"So, how long are you ladies here for?" Mason said, his eyes completely on Jenny.

"One entire month," Jenny said, enunciating each word. Then, she smiled.

A lightbulb flickered on in the hallway just as the last of the light disappeared in the sky. Reggae music wafted down the hallway, and the vignette comforted Steph. She took another drink of her beer and felt the alcohol whizz in her veins.

Jenny continued, "Unfortunately, we got here too late today to be able to jump straight in the water."

"Yeah, but Jen, we fucking made it," Steph said, and she stretched her beer past Ian and Mason to clink bottles with Jenny. They both let out a chuckle as their clumsy "cheers" caused a small amount of beer to splash onto the table.

As she drew her hand back, she brushed Ian's warm arm, and she would have sworn she felt him flex. Looking up at her, he smiled, and she grinned back with a tooth-filled smile. She was happy and felt amazing. She could finally relax.

The last few days leading up to the trip, Steph had been in the heightened state Jenny had always called "The Planner." She did what she had always done: made a long list of how many transitions her trip would take. She still had the itinerary locked in her brain. The trip to Jauh was broken down into five sections.

#1 Taxi ride to the airport (30 minutes)
#2 Flight to Singapore (8 hours flight time)
#3 Flight to Medan, Indonesia (1.5 hours)
#4 Flight to Jauh (50 minutes)
#5 Taxi van to the Break (~~5 hours~~ 2 hours)

Five steps that amounted to a very long day. Of course, these times only included actual traveling time—they didn't cover showing up early, layovers, and other trivial pieces that made each step its own organism. Steph thought back to two years ago, when they had been in Jauh and she had spent the entire day planning each of Jenny's steps back to the States. That trip had consisted of seventeen mini-trips over two days. So five microorganism trips weren't too bad. A cold beer to end this day along with one of her best friends at one of her favorite places was the perfect ending to a five-part trip. The hot guys were a lucky bonus.

Ian reached into his pocket and took out a joint. Lighting it up, he took a hit then handed it to Steph. Jenny and Mason were in deep conversation, and the music seemed a little louder. Steph propped her bare feet on the rim of the balcony and saw that her pedicure still looked fresh and new. *Yes, life is perfect,* she thought as she took a drag off the joint.

CHAPTER TWO
"DUA"

Later that night, Jenny readjusted her yellow bikini top and looked at her reflection in the dingy mirror. *All that running has paid off,* she thought as she pulled up her board shorts and snapped them shut. They immediately slid down until they hit her hips bones and rested comfortably. She beamed. She was truly in the best shape of her life.

The voices from the balcony grew louder along with the music. Jenny gave herself a final look and smiled. Satisfied, she grabbed one of the bottles of vodka she and Steph had bought in Singapore and sauntered back onto the balcony to join the little group that had gathered. This first night on Jauh was getting more interesting by the minute.

Ian, Mason, and Steph were still settled around the table, as they'd been before she'd gone to change. But now, Hamden and some other local boys that Steph and Jenny knew were lounging against the balcony rails. One of the local boys, Rio, smiled at Jenny and then laughed when he saw the bottle of booze in her hand. A whooping went up from the table as Ian and Mason now noticed the vodka, too.

"Alright, boys, calm down," Jenny said, and she opened the bottle. She took a gulp of the vodka straight from the bottle, feeling the burning in her throat. "*Oi,* that is strong!" She handed the bottle over to Steph, who mimicked Jenny's gulp and reaction.

Jenny felt a nudge at her side and looked up at Hamden, who handed her a freshly rolled joint. He still had his sunglasses on even though it was nearly eleven at night. Jenny saw new wrinkles stroke his cheeks. She wondered briefly if two years had aged her as much but then thought better of it. Hamden's lifestyle as a dealer for tourists might be relaxed, but this tropical sun could really do some damage. Anyway, he was about ten years older than her.

Rio also surprised Jenny; he was now married and even had a baby boy. He was young, though, not even twenty years old, and was still known as the "magazine boy" to the tourists. Every day, he touted around books and magazines to buy or trade with the foreigners. Of course, he hung out for the nightly drinks and joints, too.

The full moon rose over the water, and Jenny remembered why she had changed into her board shorts. "Full moon surfing!"

"I'm *not* going," Steph said, taking a deep drag off the joint. Steph had one of those raspy voices that sounded like she had just laughed really hard, and it never failed to warm Jenny to hear it.

"Let's go!" Mason stood up and did an impromptu break dancing move. Jenny giggled but enjoyed watching his shirtless torso six-pack abs wiggle around. He was probably around 6'5—definitely the fittest tall guy Jenny had ever seen. Most guys that were tall were lanky and hunched over, but not Mason. He held up his posture, and he was extremely muscular—not waiflike in the least. *Yum,* thought Jenny.

Hamden let out a chuckle. "I'm staying right here."

Jenny couldn't help but notice as Hamden's attention settled on Steph. Hamden and Steph had been somewhat of an item during their previous visits. Jenny reckoned that was probably because they had always stayed at Auntie Lorrie's losmen before, and only the local guys were allowed up there. Jenny shrugged her shoulders. She was sure that Steph would end up shagging Ian for the next few weeks as he was the single, pro-surfer Australian, rather than Hamden, the married, skinny Indonesian.

"Okay, Mason. I guess it's just us two."

ಬ

The water was inky black, and as Mason glanced up at Jenny, he appreciated how the glow of the moon created a halo around her. Jumping off the rocks, he landed on his surfboard in the water. He looked back and saw Jenny jump onto her board and into the water.

Bam! "Aaagh!" A fish jumped out of the water and hit Jenny on the chest and then flailed back into the water. That certainly interrupted the magical mood.

"What the fuck?" Mason couldn't believe what had just happened.

"I've never…," Jenny said, and then they both started laughing.

Jenny stroked hard with her arms in the water to catch up to Mason and then passed him. Mason watched her and couldn't help but notice how her back was nicely sculpted as she paddled away. As if she could feel him looking at her, she turned her head back at him and grinned.

"I can barely see where I am going—I can only hear the waves," she said.

He took a couple of long strokes and easily caught up with her. "I got ya," he said. This was not his first time out surfing during a full moon, so he settled in and let his breathing deepen. "Just listen."

Keeping quiet, they both kept paddling with their arms, laying prone on their boards. Sure enough, there was the distinct sound of water sucking backwards nearby. "Turn your board!" he yelled out, recognizing the sound as meaning a rogue larger wave was behind them.

"Oh shit, oh shit, oh shit!" Jenny did as she was told, and the moon glared off the now-clear face of the wave. Giving her a little shove, Mason then quickly turned his board and pushed the top forcefully down to duck-dive under the wave. When he popped up, he could hear the soft roar of water and saw Jenny's blonde hair glowing in the moonlight; she had made it and was riding the wave. He then felt the water sucking back and knew the second wave in the set was about to hit, so he reached down deep in the water and stroked hard. Although the moon was out, the darkness provided a quiet that enveloped him deeply as he slid down on his board on the lip of the wave and then bounced effortlessly to his feet. He squatted down to put pressure on his board to go quicker. He had to connect to the feel of the wave as he couldn't see anything any longer; the moon must have gone behind a cloud. Twisting his abs back and forth, he pushed down more into his squat and rode the wave as if he was painting it with broad strokes of a paintbrush. The euphoric feeling of the ride was amplified by the dope, booze, and Jenny. She was gorgeous, and the past several hours had been more fun than he had had in years. He was exhilarated in this moment.

"Woo-hoo!" Jenny yelled.

Mason couldn't agree with her more.

CHAPTER THREE
"TIGA"

A humid breeze swept through the open window and pressed the sheet against Jenny's sweaty skin. Kicking her leg, she managed to get the sheet off, but she was now awake. The entire room was sticky, and the sun was already streaming in. A rooster crowed, and Jenny rubbed her temples. *Too much vodka and weed.*

At least one thing was pleasant. She let her gaze settle on Mason, who was snoring softly next to her on the small bed. He lay on his back, and his long, muscular arms made a pillow for his head as they were clasped behind him. He was completely naked except for the sheet covering parts of his body she would rather see. At least his chest and the top of his hips were exposed, and she let her gaze settle on him for a few pleasant minutes. The night before had been…luscious. The two had been an item for about a week now, and Jenny was loving every minute of it. Everything on his body was long and hard. Everything.

Feeling better already, she leaned over the bed and picked up the running clothes left out the night before. Jenny loved the fact that Mason slept in so she could go for a quick run before joining Steph for a surf. As she finished tying up her running shoes, Mason grunted and turned on his side, his arm- pillow coming undone.

Carefully, Jenny turned the doorknob and tiptoed into the hallway. The rickety wooden boards creaked under her feet, and the rooster crowed again with what seemed like renewed vigor. *Oh, screw it,* she thought and bounded down the stairs. As soon as her feet hit the ground, she leapt forward in a jog, desperately wanting to be away from the losmen before Adi saw her. If he saw her, he would undoubtedly say a loud, *"Selamat pagi!"* "Good morning" was always said so painstakingly loud in the Bahasa Indonesian language. Of course, the smile that went along with "selamat pagi" would be a huge grin.

It never ceased to amaze Jenny how early Indonesians woke up. She totally got it, though—it was the coolest part of the day in the early morning, so it made sense to be up and around, wide awake by six in the morning. She kind of resented it, though, as her morning runs were private. It was exhausting to be jolted out of her zone to say the mandatory "selamat pagi" with a loud voice and huge grin to everyone she saw. She couldn't pull the Western, "I've got my earphones in and am not even going to look in your direction when I run" attitude. That was too rude here. So even if she did have her iPod blasting music, she still had to say the necessary good morning and smile.

As she jogged further down the road, she reached a fork in the road and turned left, picking up her pace. A surfer guy was walking down the street towards her. He seemed so out of place off the beach and walking on the street. She gave him a nod (but not a "selamat pagi"), and he smiled broadly back at her. He seemed interesting. She wondered why he was up walking and not surfing.

Not looking back over her shoulder, she picked up the speed as she raced past rice paddy fields and started up the hill. She loved this route. When her lungs started to feel like they couldn't take it anymore, and her quads burned, the hill would level out, and she would enter a quiet village with ancient stone houses on either side of the road. With the euphoria of the running high and pushing herself hard, the houses would appear surreal, and the people out and about wouldn't bother her any longer. She would be truly awake.

The sweat trickled out of her pores, and she shook out her arms. Yep, this morning, she would make a personal best time. Glancing at her watch, she picked up her stride and tucked into herself, willing her legs to go faster and the vodka to leave her body.

ଔ

Steph let out a short groan. The humidity was especially heavy this morning and hung in her room like a heavy, wool blanket. Hamden was sleeping soundly next to her. She knew she should wake him up and urge him out of her room before everyone in the losmen started to stir, but she just couldn't bring herself to watch him sneak out and go back to his wife.

His wife must know that he screwed around; he had been gone all night. Steph brushed her curly hair off her forehead to get some relief from the heat, but it didn't help. She noticed she was getting hotter lying there thinking about Hamden's wife and realized with a jolt that she was falling for him again. Maybe Hamden's wife *didn't* suspect anything, because there were hardly any Western girls on Jauh, and being out dealing dope all night with the Western guys was normal, because that's how he made his living. And just maybe that was more of the truth. Maybe, just maybe, Steph was the exception and the only affair. That thought almost scared Steph more than the thought of just being a fling. She closed her eyes and let her mind drift to the thought of actually being with Hamden in a real relationship. The warm fuzzy feeling was fleeting as the image she had created of his wife's abruptly appeared in her mind, and then the logistics of where they would live crowded in, and then what she would tell her parents, the difficulty of Hamden getting a job in Australia, and...*thud, thud, thud.*

The sound of someone walking up the stairs made Steph jump, and she opened her eyes. Through the thin wooden walls, she realized it was Jenny's distinct footsteps now coming down the hallway. Jenny was always the first one awake, and Steph usually tried to shoo Hamden out while Jenny was on her run, but apparently, Steph had slept in this morning. She could tell Jenny had just gotten back from her morning run as she could hear Jenny's loud breathing and the muffled music coming from her headphones.

Steph had gotten lucky in the "rock, paper, scissors" contest and had won the front room, which had the view of the ocean, but it was also right next to the balcony. In the morning, that was where people ate; during the day, it was where people lay in hammocks and had lunch; and at night, it was the dining room table and bar. Sneaking Hamden in and out was getting to be a real pain. It was times like these when Steph regretted winning the bet and tried to think of a plausible reason to get out of the best room.

"Hey…," Steph whispered next to Hamden's ear.

"Hmmm?" Hamden blinked his eyes open. Smiling at Steph, he reached over and grabbed her breast.

Steph slapped his hand away and let out a laugh that quickly turned into a cough. *I've got to quit smoking…again,* she thought and got out of bed.

Hamden, now sitting up on his elbows, looked her over and smiled again. "Shhh…." He motioned with his index finger over his mouth.

Steph flipped him off, and he let out a snort. Now, it was Steph's turn to hold her finger up and whisper "Shhh."

Opening the door an inch, Steph could see Jenny doing some yoga stretches on the balcony. Her headphones were in her ears, but Steph couldn't hear music any longer. As Jenny went into downward dog, she looked at Steph between her legs and smiled. Steph nervously smiled back and then shut the door, retreating into her room.

"Okay, it's just Jenny. You need to go," she whispered to Hamden.

Hamden, now dressed in his clothes from the night before, walked over and kissed Steph hard on the mouth. "Okay, you go out and distract her by standing by the balcony, and I'll leave. Just keep the door open."

How did this strategy come to him so easily? He must do this more often than she thought.

If Adi saw him leaving, at least Hamden could just give him a little dope, and he wouldn't say a word. Auntie Lorrie would have screamed this affair to the entire village, including Hamden's wife, if she had ever seen him sneaking out of Steph's room. During her last visit to Jauh, Hamden had stayed in her hot room the entire day because Auntie Lorrie was outside cooking and doing laundry all day. Even with the balcony room, Steph still had a better situation at Adi's.

Steph adjusted her tank top and opened the door. Jenny was in some other pose now and looking towards the balcony, so it was easy for Steph to saunter over in front of her and start talking.

"Good run?" Steph asked and leaned against the railing.

Jenny took out her headphones and brushed sweat off her forehead. "Yep, it was amazing, but it's super muggy today."

"I know. The humidity is suffocating." Steph said, trying not to look up as Hamden tiptoed out of her room. The boards creaked, and Steph cleared her throat and began talking loudly. "So, which beach do you want to surf today? We could go down to the one with the sandbar, if you like."

"Ah, yeah, either one. I just want some coffee and a quick breakfast first." Getting untangled from a yoga pose that Steph couldn't name, Jenny walked over next to Steph.

They both looked out across the beach, which spanned their entire view. Small, clean waves broke at the big wave, and a few guys were already paddling out.

"Selamat pagi!" Adi said and set down two coffees. *Kopi Aceh.* This was a type of brewed coffee like a French press. Unfortunately, Jauh was a Christian island, so they didn't brew marijuana into it like on the Muslim mainland.

Jenny grinned. "*Terima kasi*—thank you! You are a rock star, Adi."

"Yes, the absolute best," Steph said, and she searched Adi's eyes to see if there was any sign that he had seen Hamden leave the losmen. Adi only smiled back brightly, so she took a drink of her coffee and relaxed her shoulders. The strong, bitter taste made her stomach relax, and instantly, she wanted a cigarette. Scanning the table, she saw a pack of Marlboro Lights and grabbed a smoke.

Before coming to Indonesia on this holiday, she had lost twenty pounds and had miraculously quit smoking for three weeks. She had been so proud of herself. As soon as she and Jenny had met up in Singapore and grabbed some free samples of alcohol, though, that had all changed. They had gone outside and smoked cigarettes and ordered a plate of chicken wings. And now, back on Jauh, it felt like second nature to hang out on the balcony of a losmen, drink kopi Aceh, and smoke a cigarette. This was what it was all about. That and, of course, the wave. The Shangri-La of the surfing world.

"If you could bring us toast and eggs, that would be great," Jenny said. Adi gave a slight bow and walked away.

One of the surfers who had been paddling out slid down the face of a wave on his tiny surfboard. Seemingly effortlessly, he popped up on his surfboard and began carving out the virgin wave. Except when the girls were out surfing themselves, this was to be their view all day. Steph let out a quiet sigh.

"So, you seem like a girl who got laid last night," Jenny said unceremoniously, making Steph jump. A splash of coffee dropped on the railing.

Steph let out a laugh. "Whoa, what?" She coughed. "That would be you. How was your night with Mason?"

"Well, yes, the sex is quite good." Jenny laughed. Blushing made her look younger than her thirty years. "I mean, you know when they say size matters?" Jenny whispered and looked up at Steph, as if telling her a secret. "They're right."

CHAPTER FOUR

"EMPAT"

The sundrenched beach glistened in the heat. Jenny pushed her hands against her surfboard and lazily kicked her feet around until she was facing Steph. "We need sunglasses with straps on them so they stay on our heads."

Steph, also sitting on her surfboard, shielded her eyes with one hand and peered out across the ocean. They had apparently picked the wrong break to go to as the sand-bottom beach was flat today.

It was always hard to get back into surfing. Neither girl was especially good, so the big wave in front of their losmen was intimidating—especially with pro surfers dropping in on every wave. They would only surf the big wave up to about three feet—anything bigger than that scared both girls, so they would end up surfing in the whitewash (which was usually a good two to three feet anyway) or at the sand beach.

"Yeah, no kidding. Remember when Audrey wore her sunglasses out the back of the big wave?"

Both girls let out a laugh.

"Oh, shit, that was funny. She was so stoned and just paddled out the back of those big-ass seven-foot waves wearing her sunglasses."

That had been when they were staying at Auntie Lorrie's. Steph and Jenny had been drinking their morning kopi Aceh and enjoying a cigarette when they'd noticed one of the surfers was their friend Audrey. The thing was that Audrey was high the entire time she was in Jauh. Even Hamden, who dealt and smoked weed all the time, was shocked by Audrey's consumption. Audrey, barely a surfer at all, had tumbled over sideways as a wave pummeled her, and, when she popped up, her sunglasses were gone.

"That wave just came out of nowhere! That must've been such a shock for her." Jenny swirled her hand in the warm water, cupping a palm of water, and tipped it over her shoulders, which were dry already.

"Speaking of rogue waves, we just got lucky," Steph said, dropping to her stomach and turning her surfboard around.

Glancing up, Jenny saw a nice set of waves finally rolling in. Using her hands and feet like rotors, Jenny turned her board so it was facing the beach. Then, she dropped down to her stomach and paddled with long strokes. "Party wave!"

ॐ

Jenny's arms tightened around Mason's waist as the scooter bounced up and down over the potholes in the road. He let out a smile that she couldn't see and sped up.

"Turn right on the next road," Jenny said, and Mason felt her warm breath on his ear.

Mason did as he was told, and they drove to the bottom of the small mountain. They jolted to a stop, and Jenny's arms slid down his hips momentarily, and then she got off the bike.

"Okay, sex at the summit?" Jenny said in that confident tone she had. That tone made her the sexiest holiday fling he had ever had. Her hands were propped on her hips, and she tilted her head to the side, waiting for his reply.

For some reason, Mason was feeling shy and overwhelmed by this beauty. Although she was only five feet, four inches and about 115 pounds, she emanated a sexy courage that was rare for a woman.

"I'll race you," Mason said.

Grabbing the machete from the back of the bike, he strapped it around his back. Jenny was already sprinting towards a grassy area that looked like a promising quasi-trail to the top. Taking large strides, Mason quickly caught up and then overtook her up the foot of the mountain. He bounded up with Jenny at his heels.

Finally, when they were near the top, he slowed down to a labored jog as he entered a patch of thick sword grass. Feeling the grass slice through his skin like little papercuts, he let out a yell. "Ouch!"

He heard Jenny's heavy breathing behind him and turned around. "Use the machete," she puffed out and put her hands on her knees, taking in deep breaths. Unstrapping the machete, Mason thrashed it through the grass and felt the satisfaction of the patch being torn apart. He continued in this manner, thinking about his reward at the top.

Luckily, they found the top had barren little parts and an amazing view of a large harbor. They both stared in relative silence with only their thick breathing creating any noise.

"Wow," Jenny said. She took a bottle of water out of a small backpack and took a drink, then handed the bottle to Mason.

Taking a deep swallow, Mason enjoyed the water saturating his body, even though it wasn't cold any longer. He had pushed himself up this hill with more gusto than ever. But, knowing Jenny ran every morning, he had to dig in deep and remember his leg muscle memory. He ran a bit in Australia, but in Jauh, his workouts were almost always surfing…that is, until Jenny had arrived.

During the lull of the day, between the best surfing of the morning and evening, they had gotten into the habit of setting off on little adventures. Usually, their adventures included physical activities. Yesterday, they had hiked up to a small village where there was a large waterfall and had jumped in from the top. It had been refreshing to swim in cold, fresh water. Of course, a lot of their outings included sex, since mostly they went to secluded areas. Today was no different.

Screwing the top back onto the water, Mason set it down. Jenny had already taken a sarong out of the backpack and was sitting down on it. "I'm still sweating like a gazillion ton of water," she said.

Mason sat down next to her, "Yes, and you will be sweating even more in a minute."

He kissed her deeply and passionately, feeling her lean back until she lay flat on her back. Hovering over her, he kissed her harder and felt her legs naturally unfold underneath him so there was a space in between for him. He settled there and grinded up against her, growing harder.

ജ

Jenny felt like her skin was crawling. She scratched again, then took a drink of her beer.

"You alright?" Steph said, then let out a deep, gravely laugh as Jenny started scratching her backside.

"Those fucking mosquitos," Jenny said and scratched again.

Steph snorted with laughter. "Well, that's what you get for having sex on the top of a mountain in the tropics."

Jenny smiled. "Oh, *butt* it was worth it. Pun intended."

Steph shook her head side to side and grinned. "Oh, Jenny, you are scoring big time on this holiday."

"It's only one guy. Just one lovely guy." She let out a sigh.

"And he wants to go to Belgium with you?" Steph's eyes narrowed, and Jenny felt exposed.

Once this holiday was over, Jenny was moving to Brussels to work on her master's degree. Mason had been enamored with Jenny's move and kept hinting about not wanting to go back to Australia. He had even gone so far as to say that he could get a job in Brussels doing some sort of construction work.

Jenny *was* having the time of her life with Mason, but it was partly because he was a holiday fling, not a serious live-in boyfriend. Plus, as much as she didn't want to be a snob, he was an uneducated surfer who was seven years her junior, and Jenny was looking forward to meeting intellectual guys her age. A university in Europe seemed the perfect place for that scenario. Moving to a different country with a hot fling she had only known a couple of weeks seemed premature to say the least, no matter how great the sex and daily adventures were.

"Yeah, well, then there's that…I just can't see it happening."

"Definitely not," Steph said.

Jenny looked out at the water just in time to see Mason catch a great wave. His muscular body flexed as he put pressure on his board and caught some air. He really was something to watch. Ian caught the next wave, and Jenny noticed how cut his body was, too. He was probably in his 40s and was more of a quiet guy who read a lot on the balcony. He was perfect for Steph, but somehow Steph and Ian never seemed to be alone on the balcony, which was strange since Jenny and Mason were off gallivanting every day.

"But, if he ever wanted to meet up here the next time we come, well, I'd be up for that. You know, it's too bad that he doesn't live here—that would be even easier." Jenny smiled coyly as Steph's cheeks grew red. Jenny knew her assumption was right. "Kind of like Hamden."

"W-hat?" Steph choked on her beer and set it down. "What do you mean?"

"Don't act like I don't know," Jenny giggled. "Come on, you haven't slept with Ian, and you hide out in your room sometimes...when there is this view if you just open your door! Plus, Hamden comes around every night and gives you the *look*. I mean, even when he keeps his sunglasses on at night, I can tell he is giving you the *look*."

Steph lit up a cigarette, dropping any pretense. "He does? He gives me a look?"

Oh shit. Steph was in deep if she wanted reassurance of "the look."

"Why haven't you told me?" Jenny asked, now feeling like the shit friend who had been too caught up in her own holiday fling to even know about her friend's affair.

"Well, your shagging is just so much more interesting, and let's face it: Hamden has a wife, and I am kind of ashamed." Steph let out a groan. "What am I am doing?"

Lighting up a smoke, Jenny inhaled deeply, and, as she exhaled slowly, she looked at Steph evenly. "It's been the entire time, hasn't it?"

Steph closed her eyes tightly. "Yes," she said in a small voice. "Since...the first night. He is just so good in bed."

"And what about when we leave next week? Is there anything more?"

"No, it's nothing like that. It is strictly a fling. I mean he lives here, is married, and deals dope. There is no hope for us, nor would I want that. It's just about the sex."

Jenny knew that Steph was convincing herself, but she also knew that, when you had chemistry with someone, logic didn't enter the chambers of the heart.

"Okay." Jenny let it go at that. She knew that Steph would talk to her more about it when she was ready.

Looking up, Jenny saw that Ian and Mason were walking back, surfboards under their arms. She and Steph had needed this evening. Usually, they would be at the beach surfing, too, but tonight, they had decided to stay on the balcony and have some beer and a chat. Plus, Jenny—and probably Steph, too—was sore from all the sex and wanted to relax and get a little drunk.

Jenny scratched her bottom again and then picked up her beer. "Well, cheers, my friend—to both of us getting laid."

Relief washed over Steph's face, and she let out a laugh. "I guess secret indoor sex has some benefits."

Hearing footsteps up the stairs, Jenny looked over her shoulder and saw Ian and Mason—both wet and strong. They were chatting so hopefully hadn't heard any of Steph and Jenny's conversation.

"You guys rocked out some of those waves," Jenny yelled. Mason looked up and smiled at Jenny, then, putting his surfboard down, he ran down the hallway. Swooping Jenny up into his arm, he kissed her hard on the mouth. The water made Jenny's nipples harden. "Put me down! Now I'm all wet," she said, letting out a laugh.

"Okay, my love," Mason said in that accent Jenny loved so much. "But first, you have to be honest with me. You are not wearing a bra, are you?"

Jenny's eyes widened, and Steph let out a groan. Shaking her head no, Jenny smiled.

Setting her down, Mason mouthed, "I didn't think so."

He was staring directly at her chest. It didn't help that her halter top was white, so it was transparent now that it was wet. Instead of hiding herself, Jenny pushed her chest out more and took another drag off her cigarette.

"So now that you are wet, you must need a shower, too," Mason said.

"Good thinking, but actually, it's just a bit damp, and it's cooling me off. Plus, we are having a lovely evening of girl time."

Mason pushed his hand through his sandy-blond hair and stared at Jenny for a moment. "Alright, you enjoy your time. But I will be back in a minute, so you will need to have some boy time, too."

He turned and walked away, shaking out his hair some more so that water sprayed onto the hallway walls. Jenny took a swig off her beer as she watched him walk down the hallway until he disappeared into his (well, it had kind of become *their* room). She just loved the way his strong back curved and was built from all the paddling while he surfed.

"Oh, Jen, you really are something," Steph said, taking a drag off her cigarette and blowing the smoke out into the darkening sky. They heard both water faucets turning on in the guys' rooms.

"I know, I have this weird confidence...but, it's because it is a *fling*, Steph." Jenny gestured towards Ian's room. "You should really try out the menu. How often do you get to have sex with professional surfers on a remote tropical island? I mean, this is it, Steph. We aren't getting any younger. Skinny, older, and married Indonesian men just don't quite compare."

Steph winced and twisted off the top from a new bottle of vodka, the last one they had left from their loot at the Singapore airport. Jenny knew she was pushing some buttons for Steph to be getting out the hard stuff this early in the evening.

"I know. It would be so easy if Hamden just didn't come around," Steph said.

Jenny grabbed some glasses off the corner table, then stood up, feeling her buzz strengthen. She walked over to the cooler to get a chaser for the vodka. The hangover after the first night of drinking vodka straight from the bottle had taught her a lesson.

"Yeah, that's a bitch," Jenny said. "But just be a grown woman and flirt with Ian. It's like Hamden has these magical powers over you."

"I know!" Steph said. "It's so weird. I see Ian, and I run, because I don't want..." Steph bit her lip and looked at the dark sky.

"You don't want what?" Jenny popped opened a can of Coke and took a sip as she walked back to the table.

Letting out a tight sigh, Steph looked directly at Jenny. "I don't want Hamden to get jealous."

Jenny spit out the Coke in a spray across the table. "*You* don't want *him* to get jealous? He's the one who is married!"

The water turned off in Ian's room, and he started to hum. Both girls covered their mouths with their hands, realizing he'd probably heard their increasingly loud conversation.

"Oops," Jenny whispered.

"I mean…ah, that's what you should tell your friend," Jenny said loudly and then shrugged her shoulders.

Steph started laughing, grabbed the soda from Jenny, and poured the Coke into two glasses, then picked up the bottle of vodka.

Jenny wondered if Ian had heard the conversation. Apparently, they were both a little bit more drunk than they'd thought, which meant they were talking louder than they thought.

And then, as if matters couldn't get worse, Hamden walked down the hallway.

"Right on time," Jenny said.

Instead of pouring the vodka into the glasses, Steph took a long swig from the bottle.

Yes, this is going to be a long night, Jenny thought.

CHAPTER FIVE

"LIMA"

The ball ricocheted off the side pocket of the pool table with a crack. Mason felt the sweat sting his armpits, so he stretched his arms over his head to cool off.

"Your turn, hot stuff," Jenny said as she leaned on her now-standing pool stick.

"You're kicking my ass," he said.

Jenny let out a laugh. "Hardly, I just missed that one."

"I know, but it was a crazy good shot—even if you didn't get it in. Not to mention there are only three of your solid balls left on the table and six of my stripes."

She smiled. "Aw, is someone being a sore loser before they lose? I'm sorry, baby. Should I play a little less aggressively?"

Even though Jenny had on no make-up, her green eyes were bright against her dark tan and her sun-streaked blonde hair. She was the most natural beauty he had ever seen. And then there was the sex. He had never had such an intense relationship with someone he had just met. He wanted this one to last. And now, she had the scholarship to Belgium.

That was what had made her so confident at pool tonight. They had played pool before, and she had gotten a few shots in but mostly just smack-talked him without being able to defend her cocky attitude. Today, though, she was slamming the balls in left and right.

A few hours prior, he had heard Jenny shrieking with joy from the downstairs "internet cafe." Adi had the only losmen on Jauh to have very intermittent internet and the only computer that you could use as it was a good-ole dial-up internet connection. Mason had run down the wooden stairs, feeling the entire losmen shake, to see what Jenny was screaming about.

"You alright?" he had asked, out of breath.

"I got it!" Jenny had yelled, already standing up and dancing around. "I got the scholarship!"

Mason had automatically swept Jenny up into his arms and kissed her hard. "Baby, that's great!" She had been so nervous talking about the scholarship, saying it would make the world of difference to her to be able to breathe a little easier, not racking up a huge student loan living in Europe.

He still couldn't believe she was leaving for Belgium so soon. Only another week on the island with him. If only he could convince her to let him go with her. So far, he had hinted a bit here and there, but they hadn't had THE conversation yet.

"You deserve it," he had said and had put her down gently.

Then, they had joined hands and run to Adi's scooter.

"Where to, lucky girl?" he had asked, feeling her rush of excitement settle into his nerves.

"Somewhere fun!"

After speeding past the beach, where they had met, they'd ended up at the rickety, open air pool hall. Four older Indonesian men, who seemed to be permanent structures in the pool hall, sat nursing beers. The radio in the corner had a soccer game on, and the men looked up briefly at Mason and Jenny, then resumed a loud conversation. It was the only place to really *go to,* and after being in Jauh for nearly a month, Mason really felt like a night out on the town.

As the two easily settled into grabbing their pool sticks and setting up the game, Mason felt a quiet, comfortable ease with Jenny.

Bending over, Mason concentrated on his striped eleven ball. He rammed the white cue ball with his pool stick, and it jumped up, then went off course.

A small *yippee!* escaped from Jenny, and she swayed from side to side. "Sorry, Mason. But I'm going to break out the big guns now."

Mason couldn't help but laugh. She was so darn cute wearing that oversized white sundress that hung around her body in a way that made her slim body so easy to see. Sashaying over to the pool table, Jenny bent down, and Mason could clearly see down the front part of her dress as it hung down, nearly displaying her nipples. She had stayed on her trend of not wearing a bra for the last couple of weeks, and that was one thing that he could tell for sure based on the dress. Automatically, Mason glanced up to the bar where the men sat, but they were too enamored with their discussion to pay any attention to the *bules.*

Jenny smacked the cue ball, which rammed her ball into the side pocket and then slowed down and set her up perfectly for her next shot.

"Damn, you do have some big guns," Mason said, glancing down her dress.

Jenny readjusted her dress. "Well, they aren't that big, but they get the job done."

౸

Some days passed, and Jenny still couldn't believe her luck on this holiday.

This is his first actual date? she thought, both satisfied and thrown off guard. It was something they had discovered during one of their long chats: Mason had never actually gone on a date. Of course, he'd had plenty of hook-ups and relationships before, but he had never been on a *date*.

She couldn't stand that Mason, in his early 20s and with his 6'4" of hotness, had never had a proper date before, and, at the same, she was nervous that *she* was his first.

The full moon sparkled in the sky, and it dawned on Jenny that it had been exactly one month since she had hooked up with Mason. It was fitting that they should be celebrating their one-month anniversary with a proper date.

Today, when he'd awkwardly asked her out on a proper date, she had blushed but then said yes. He'd then asked her if she would lead him to a place in the reef that she had been talking about. Of course, Jenny had to show the way since he had never joined her on her morning runs to see this place, which seemed a bit odd for a first date, but it was what it was.

They walked in relative silence until the moon started to rise, and then they both drifted to a stop. The full moon hovered over the ocean like a good omen. The night instantly became enchanting as a cool breeze rustled the leaves of the palm trees, taking with it the dense humidity of the last month. It was then that the date turned into a date…and Mason automatically reached over and held her hand in his. This small gesture was more impactful to Jenny than all their multiple sex positions had ever been. Then, to make it even more intimate, Mason squeezed her hand.

Jenny risked a look at Mason, and he was staring at her. It wasn't the usual lustful stare he gave her; it was something else. That something else scared Jenny. Then, he pulled her in against his chest and wrapped his arms around her. Breathing in his now-familiar scent, Jenny allowed her eyes to close and her mind to dream of the "what-ifs." She knew this was what he wanted, but she also knew that, when she was in her early 20s, she'd wanted things that probably weren't the best, either. But she wanted to allow herself to have the dream for a moment at least. To feel love blossom and grow into risky places of commitment.

Letting out a sigh, she opened her eyes and released her embrace.

"Come on, we're almost there," she said, tugging at his hand to follow her.

They continued down past the last losmen and then onto the deserted part of the beach that Jenny knew went on for another few miles. The grass patch wasn't too much farther, though. Once they rounded a slight curve, the only light was from the moon.

"Here it is," Jenny said as they neared the patch of grass, which glowed under the light of the moon. It was just as she remembered it. A small oval of beautiful, full grass sat amongst a section of the reef and looked like a tiny floating island. They walked out carefully across the exposed reef that drifted up to the shore.

"Wow, it's just like you said," Mason said when they reached the grass, and then he took off his backpack. "This is amazing."

Jenny let out a laugh. "Right? I am so glad you think so, too. It's such a strange but perfect sight."

The waves crashed at the edges, but they were safe in the middle of the grass. Mason set his backpack down and opened it up. *Damn, he's prepared,* Jenny thought as he began taking things out. First, he laid down a blanket and then began spreading items out—some snacks, his portable speaker, an iPod, four beers, and a joint. The tunes of *The Black Seeds* wafted into the air as he plugged his iPod into the speaker. The melodic music combined with the beauty of the full moon created a luscious moment.

Jenny reached over and lit up the joint, breathing in the earthy and sweet taste. Leaning over, she connected her lips with Mason's and exhaled the smoke into his mouth. His tongue twirled around hers, and she felt the soft thickness. She knew this was a perfect moment. She knew there might be some backlash to her recklessness. Maybe a broken heart. Or a broken promise to herself. But she also knew this was a moment of complete vividness. Of complete life.

Afterword

The Break is a fictionalized memoir based on my time in Indonesia. Characters are not necessarily based on real people, events have been dramatized, names have been changed, and the histories of characters have been changed. This book was not written to cause a scandal or offend any person, culture, or religion. The hope is that this book will serve as an encouragement for open dialogue while enriching a universal sharing of emotions through a unique story.

The Break is a part of the Sojourning Soul Series. You can find other novels at www.sojourningsoulseries.com. *Handful of Smoke* is the final novel in the series and can be found at www.handfulofsmoke.com. Get the first two chapters of *Handful of Smoke* for free at www.handfulofsmoke.com.

Acknowledgements

No piece or writing, no matter how long or how short, is ever easy to write, edit, edit some more, write some more, edit, publish, and ultimately sell. The entire process is like riding a wave. Just braving the waters in the creation of a piece of literary art takes the support of many. I want to thank the following people for their support in allowing me to be vulnerable and create my art: first and foremost, my daughter, Isabella Rustick, who inspires me to always be more and take risks; Deborah Ellen, my mother who helps watch Isabella so I can write at dingy bars or fancy hotels; Jean Claude de Cayette, who has been a believer in my work; Jason Salas, who is ALWAYS my first beta reader and gives amazing criticism in a very nurturing way; Amber Word, who is such an encourager and accountability partner; Claudia Clement, for her down-to-earth and guru-like wise suggestions; Leone Rohr, who inspires me beyond belief and keeps me on track; Joan Awa, an author who is kicking ass and inspired me to stop procrastinating on the publication of this book; my Advanced Reader Team, who took the time to review this story and gave me amazing feedback; to all the readers who have support *Handful of Smoke* and gave me the encouragement to keep up with writing this series; Kath Magarey, who was my reunion partner on the island of Nias and inspired characters in this book – man, we had a good time!; to all my friends in Indonesia, *terima kasih!*; to my cover designer, Dr. Jay Polmar; to my editor, Hilary Gunning, who allowed me to ask her a million questions; and to that beautiful wave in Nias that has created a surf culture, a thriving economy, and now a story – mother nature rocks.

About the Author

When she's not hunched over at her laptop drinking Pinot Noir at dingy bars, you can find Erica Sand playing tag in the sand with her daughter on the beaches of Guam or pulling artists together for a creative event. Erica has traveled the world as an international expatriate professional and student and draws from her own stories and juicy tales she has heard during her travels. She is a published poet, expert grant writer, and an author who uses her own experiences to tell her stories.